Made in United States
Orlando, FL
09 September 2024

51335972R00068